and the
BIRTHDAY BANG

Justine Smith • Clare Elsom

ORCHARD

Zak Zoo lives at Number One, Africa Avenue.
His mum and dad are away on
safari, so his animal family is looking
after him. Sometimes things get a little . . .

. . . *WILD!*

Emily

Pam

Dad

Mum

Zak

Nanny
Hilda

Bob

Charlie

Grace   Mia (Zak's best friend)   Tom

Early one Saturday morning Zak Zoo got up and went to work in his shed.

Zak's animal family wanted to know what he was making, but Zak was too busy to explain.

Whatever it was, it was taking

quite a long time.

Finally, Zak Zoo finished making
Nanny Hilda's birthday present.
He wrapped it up carefully.

Then Zak went into the kitchen
to make a birthday breakfast for
Nanny Hilda.

Zak gave his nanny some small presents first. She opened them in bed with everyone sitting around her.

"That was part one of your birthday surprise," said Zak. Then he asked Nanny Hilda to go with him into the garden.

Zak and Nanny Hilda stood in the garden and unwrapped the big parcel. "This is part two of your surprise!" said Zak.

Nanny Hilda loved her present.

"I'm glad you like it," said Zak.

"Read this card to find out the last

part of your surprise."

Dear Nanny Hilda,
This is your day off.
Have fun!
Happy birthday,
Love Zak x

For one day, Nanny Hilda wouldn't have to look after Zak, or the animal family, or the house.

"Are you sure about this?" said

Mia when she stopped by.

"It's just for one day," said Zak.

He waved goodbye to his nanny

and went inside.

Suddenly, there was a loud crash at the window. It was Tom the post-bird, bringing a parcel and a letter.

Zak opened the parcel and read the letter. It was from his mum and dad.

Dear Zak,

Can you keep these fire-eggs warm in the oven?

If they hatch, let us know.

Lots of love,

Mum and Dad x

Keep →
warm

Zak was used to getting mad presents from his parents. He put the eggs in the oven and started writing a list of things to do.

TO DO LIST

1) Wash up

2) Hoover

3) Make birthday cake

19

Now Zak's list was written, he had to do everything on it. The first job was washing up. It was fun, but the kitchen got very wet.

Emily skidded . . . and fell!

"Whoops!" said Zak, helping her
up. But there was no time to mop
the floor!

The second job on Zak's list was Hoovering. But as soon as Zak turned on the Hoover, it flew around the room! It chewed up the carpet and then it ate the curtains. "Help!" said Zak.

Charlie jumped on the Hoover
and bit the bag. Dust flew out
everywhere!

"What a mess," said Zak.

"There's no time to clean up," said Zak. "We have to make Nanny Hilda's cake!"

But now they could hear a *buzzzz*! And then a *wuzzzzzz*! It was the sound of fire-eggs hatching. Then the oven door burst open.

Buzzzzz! *Wuzzzzz*! Fire-beetles zoomed around the kitchen and all around the house!

"Don't worry," said Zak. He grabbed a bucket of water.

Zak threw the water over the beetles. *Buzzzzz . . .* said the wet beetles.

At that moment the front door
opened and Nanny Hilda stepped in.
"Nanny Hilda," said Zak happily.
"We missed you so much!"

Nanny Hilda cleaned up the mess while Zak wrote to his mum and dad.

Dear Mum and Dad,

The fire-eggs hatched into fire-beetles.

It happened on Nanny Hilda's birthday.

It was a birthday bang!

Love, Zak x

Nanny Hilda made herself a birthday cake. The fire-beetles helped light the candles on the cake and everyone helped eat it.

"Happy birthday, Nanny Hilda,"
said Zak. "I'm glad you're back."

Written by Justine Smith • Illustrated by Clare Elsom

All priced at £4.99

Orchard Books are available from all good bookshops,
or can be ordered from our website: www.orchardbooks.co.uk,
or telephone 01235 827702, or fax 01235 827703.

Prices and availability are subject to change.